Stockholm Syndrome
Igor Klikovac

Translated from the Bosnian by
John McAuliffe and Igor Klikovac

smith|doorstop

Published 2018 by
Smith|Doorstop Books
The Poetry Business
Campo House
54 Campo Lane
Sheffield S12DG

Copyright © Igor Klikovac 2018
All Rights Reserved

ISBN 978-1-912196-18-0
Typeset by Utter
Printed by People for Print, Sheffield

Acknowledgements

Acknowledgements are due to the editors of the following periodicals, where some of these poems were first published: *Manchester Review*, *The North*, *Poetry Ireland Review*, *PN Review*, *Poetry (Chicago)* and *The Poetry Review*.

Smith|Doorstop Books are represented by and members of Inpress, www.inpressbooks.co.uk

Distributed by NBN International, Airport Business Centre, 10 Thornbury Road Plymouth PL6 7PP

The Poetry Business gratefully acknowledges the support of Arts Council England.

Contents

3	Elegy for the Leavers
4	The Childhood
5	Inside Job
7	Rats' Decision
8	The Youth
9	A Long Homecoming
10	Tremor
11	Friends
12	Continuum
13	Gratitude to Big Cities
14	'Fruit Pickers'
15	The Interpreter
16	The River
18	Stockholm Syndrome
20	Memory
21	Dog-sitting
22	Versions
24	Then and Now
25	Jovo
26	New Wave
28	Refurbishment
29	With Mother ...
31	Sarajevo

It would be great if, when all is said and done, it turned out that windmills are not windmills, but giants.

– Ramon Gomez de la Serna, *Aphorisms*

Elegy for the Leavers

Books devoured what was left in the open: the endings
with sad trees and smoking roofs falling off the suitcase-mound
in the back-window of a bus (a curtain limply waving
the forfeited youth goodbye), and the overload of surprise –
at the aptness of killers, at limbs still reaching for something
from the hospital rubbish. The mad courage, the boredom,
the loss of innocence through selfless thoughts; all built
into plots, published and documented fairly, save maybe
a slippery thing or two: how treason works through gravity,
and death through entanglement, particle-like; that noise
does its worst in perfect quiet …

The twice dispossessed now speak in parables, even to a postman,
guarding the virtue of the almost-nothing that remains. Someone did
leave at dawn, and saw sparrows hover in the yellow sky above the bus,
like gulls hoisted in the wake of a cruise-liner. Someone remembered
the stab of cold through the front teeth and voices of women beside
the water-pump in the mountain. And, one side of the border,
that lightning-quick outpour of mind into the harshness of land,
the sudden catch of not taking but leaving behind. This
they repeat when no one's around: it must, after all,
mean something, hope and voice-which-knows
fighting over detail. No regret, only the watchfulness of thoughts
treading backwards; like rain falling upwards –
words scoff at themselves for saying it.

The Childhood

The hard crust of our city's ice: black engine oil
and crushed kisses on cigarette butts. For a child
that water could remember was entirely logical,
and yet no less magic, and hence full of news about
what was coming. But the landscape remained grey too,
like a spent, badly-lit filming location, full of soot
and fooled people, frozen in unwitting pirouettes.

All else was too fast, deceitful or simply mute,
and directed at others. Life trickled into a shallow bowl
and disappeared before lips were brought to it. Only
the discarded and the occassional kindness of weather
could be relied on in the slippery world. Nowadays,
whenever I step into myself through a puddle, I startle;
as I did back then peering over the kitchen sill
when the winter that stretched between the buildings
got unstitched by trucks spraying salt.

Inside Job

Strange seeing what you thought forever hidden
on someone else's dinner table: a men's shoe still smoking,
unlaced by a detonation … The one today
is ceramic, its ghost rising from a smouldering butt …

A cheated death turns itself into bric-a-brac, a bit hauled
from shelf to mantel, till it gets so habit-bashed
its name can't be glued back on. It's
like being burgled by correspondence.
Was it the wind, really, that read books on your desk
while you've been away?
One day you return to the empty flat,
and only that dumb so-and-so
is grinning at you like a bailiff.

Nettle-eaters
(Birth of a Language)

Since I first heard about it, I always wanted to see
people eating pain.

Now, as they sit behind the long table, with hands stretched
out into the white tablecloth, they look like a fed-up delegation,
or an amateur club waiting for the arrival of a grandmaster.

The daydreamy looks show they are ascending into that concentration,
summoning that peace which champions and mass-murderers
walk upon. Whether they'd want to remember or forget something –
who would know, except themselves

but without that, I realise, the whole business is nothing
but a lesson in punctured expectations: noisy, too fast for the eye,
with no revelations or ontological cookie at the end. Something in fact
that pushes itself right out of one's mind

as soon as the waiters start to lift the plastic basins
and uncouple the tables. The green-tongued competitors
exit and belch thunderously in the emptying parking lot.

Rats' Decision

Dogs were slowly going rabid; cats, it was assumed,
had simply walked out. Bluebottles had a field day.
You want to see what rats are doing, a neighbour said,
if they stay it'll be bad, but it's a no-hoper if they leave.
So we played chess and waited for the sign, until
one day the others told me he'd left too, the rat-expert.

Months later, with swallows, I was on my way out
when I saw a forgotten classmate on the enemy checkpoint
go through people's papers, and thought stupidly: it's true,
everyone will have a story about the war. A borrowed name
in the pocket, my own in the coat's lining, I started praying
to the God of Rats that this doesn't become mine.

The Youth

It looked so easy. Idly overseeing crowded trams,
the stench of the merry town trickling, behind your back,
into the shallow river, paths of rust and clear light,
slanted roofs of people's lives, the singing towers,
days when no one wondered and no one asked
where you were. It took climbing all the way up
to feel it, where streets ended in Turkish courtyards
and cut-off rail tracks, green-coppered water-fountains
for the long-gone caravans. It smelt different,
the quick-footed truth of existence, and it didn't hide:
dreams hummed around it like bees, it pulled on lungs.
It wasted no voice, and only ever pointed – a sure sign
of a *sign* when you're on the lookout – there, vaguely beyond
the valley's bowl ...

Each time you'd fall for it, hurry back thinking you'd
filled pockets with a stolen future, only to be slapped down:
one look at the front door and all that borrowed freedom
crumbling like an old biscuit into a measly handful of sin ...

A Long Homecoming

Twenty-two blackbirds moving together
across the scorched grass like an unknown language
in a stranger's mouth, connected by something wholly
extraneous, incalculable. What would someone
who understands these things say, is this a dream
of distant places you crave, or something
that's already happened, long ago, while you, again,
looked somewhere else? Remember: that little boy
who, tiptoeing next to a seaside telescope,
when the eyelid on the other side lifts, is still
hearing the coin falling through the stiff guts,
picturing its pirouetting while it cries click-clack.
And afterwards recalls forever only the father
saying *look, look*, and the lump of green iron
smelling of door handles.

Tremor

It looks much simpler from a slowing airplane: kiss
the engine's last gasp with the forehead, and shred the thoughts
from five minutes before, when, briefly, it seemed that life
could again be threaded through a hole made by a needle.

One wrong word, a blast of turbulence, a moment of carelessness;
the time when a name was carried sewn into the lining of a coat
is gone. Sitting outside a cafe, nothing bad can happen to you;
you're not thinking of drunken murderers and falling planes.

Death is hidden by the finesse, the thick lace of routine. It's
in the way someone's furniture is being thrown into a truck
by the workers across the road, a dimming of noise at that
happy table every time a look falls on one empty seat and its

waiting cutlery. When drills start roaring around the corner
cups on the tin tables chatter like teeth: is that death too,
sleeping in things? Away from wars and catastrophes, it's
everywhere, flowering on rejection like a bad memory.

Between the shop-windows and smiling babies, whenever
you think how all this around you is dazzling and, more or less,
everlasting, she will rock your chair: something's changed
between you just because she's wearing gloves …

Friends

Sunday morning, the melancholy's like
going to a supermarket. A little of this,
a little of that; nothing could have worked out better.

Sitting on a concrete wall, children with grown-ups' heads
wait for someone to call out their name again,
for a football team, for unforgettable love ...

Shoulders of angels, foreheads of the future
murderers; antithesis of evil
splashed over the school's high windows ...

These days, when you run into them,
you don't know what's on the outstretched hand:
they are like pears waiting on the table – the taste

passes through them when it fancies,
or doesn't arrive at all ...

Continuum

1.

I often find Father in my laughter or the way the hand holds
a cigarette; he's still not saying much, same as back then, when we used
to bump into each other on the stairwell at dawn, one with a fishing rod
and a necklace of insects, the other – hungry for sleep. We'd say hello,
and shuffle the darkness between us with our palms down
like dominos. He looked happiest then, and I try to remember him that way;
nowadays, he seems embarrassed by all this sneaking around,
and the gimmicks he must use to remind me who it is, calling.

2.

The day I was leaving, though I hadn't told a soul, he appeared
from nowhere. Because of the strange name on my papers and all the soldiers,
he had to pretend he knew no one on the bus. He stared past my window
like he was the one being dropped in a foreign country.

3.

Our last letters touched shoulders in passing, his arriving
a few days after he was gone, mine in a pair of new shoes, together
with a pound note for his smoking debts, hidden under the insole.

4.

When he comes to visit now, at least it's clearer why one of us
had always hobbled behind. Finally, it seems, we can squeeze into
the same spot, and honour this life's haughty space-time confinement.
We take on things untroubled by possibilities, we shun choice,
our wills are perforated on a paper roll, we pass the black and white of days
always part of the same, insanely well-polished tune …

Gratitude to Big Cities

Those days when all pages are empty
are best given to running. Knowing your own name
is less important if the streets are long, and – better still –
freshly scrubbed by rain. Then it looks
like you're jumping from one façade to another,
across the outstretched necks and open windows. That alone
already feels like an improvement. Under coloured canopies,
through the courtyards of tiny churches, over pedestrian bridges
that cross no water, through the sleepy eyes of rear-mirrors,
from shop-window to shop-window, like a rambling thought.
Underneath you, the specially designed soles squeal,
and manhole covers rattle with the rhythm of images
barely catching up with their own mortality statistics …
The problem of the cracked self, thus reduced to a simple
breathing exercise, at the end simply solves itself, like
a common cold. When finally you open your eyes,
the world is again joined up by words, the light thread
which meanders through the scenery like yellow stitching
in a pair of blue-jeans, and the woman taking a jumper
from a washing-line and smelling it, while behind her
in the distance a weather balloon rises, is already
surrounded by that insatiable whiteness, the one
which never lets out what it once swallowed.

'Fruit Pickers'

Shades of green that, soon, failing eyesight will lose
behind smeared fingerprints and a film of nicotine on unwashed windows:
it's all changing quickly from rain to a downpour,
and then back again, and the lack of suitable words to describe this –
more water, less water, green as cut grass, a winter uniform green – lifts
the lid on the exuberance concealed in muteness. We hid like that, behind
walls and fences of grammar, but words always picked us off, easily ensnared
by headlights, all too predictable, slow. Why us, and not the shimmer within
hard metal, the inscrutable equations of speed and colour? The mind
goes back to those grapefruit pickers we stopped to watch from the edge
of the road, hands like pistons racking the branches, and us, waiting in vain
for someone to turn around and acknowledge our presence. In the end
we took away just that, and something behind us continued nameless.
Of it, that much was always clear, nothing more would ever be ours;
but how did the pickers know they'd departed from the solid word's will,
suddenly more a possession than the possessors? Have they too
succumbed to some kind of childlike wonder, or just worked thought-tied
until they could see themselves working?

The Interpreter

Those strange months, buried
practically unrecalled, forever
off the books now, when you lent
words to others, and they paid in
desperate trust. Nothing in common
except language, you used to think,
but still, you'd share a joke, take
a curse for a walk. Their eyes –
this is an odd, needling payback –
popped with a hopeful glint
whenever you revealed
you used to be them once ...

What reminded you? Something
said, though clearly not the same
language; words are time-warps,
so it wouldn't matter. Maybe
a sound only, a falling off, a crease;
guilt and pride clacking their heels,
each holding the door
open for the other.

The River

Standing on the bank I see them pull something black and heavy from the water, and beside a tied sack and a stiff dog unload a puddle with two limp arms and no hands. There is no one in the coat, and workers crouch and lean over the river as if itself were a question: where is the owner, did he leave the coat before or after? And was he at least a little sorry for the old coat, for the spent life? The river replies with silence, and the coat, the carcass and the secret held by the sack touch each other with profiles, like hieroglyphs. The water could not understand them, so now the hooks, the rain and human horror of dying, negotiate the meaning. Who is who, and what is what in that sentence, which, however things get shuffled, ends in a small death? Like all knots, this one too pushes the handler back, demands retracing of steps, but the semantic needs weight, it always needs some, otherwise it's nonsense or someone else's business, so it's not long before you see it pointing the finger: you're doing your own maths, so chip in, use your own numbers. It's mean of language this, how quickly a word turns personal, more or less as soon as it's abandoned by speech and touched by a thought. Not much time for a pause, just a breath really, and you're not holding an apple in a supermarket, but those Bramleys you jumped fences for as a kid. Clearly, this has its uses, and there's no other way, but still, it's inconsiderate. You don't always want to remember, not every time something's parked in front of your mind ... A soaked overcoat and a dead dog? A bloated sack? Of course, right away ... The long-lost, forgotten friends and crumbled friendships, a betrayal of trust, a lost love, an unreturned favour, an unresolved dispute, a short shrift, severe consequences, things kept from you, things you kept from others, a slide, a slip, a fall, a splash ... The whole sorry shebang, the touched bottom, the slow rot ... Or maybe just: faces of the miserable old winos from charity ads.

Underneath the words drying on the deck, the river couldn't be more different. It's steady, uniform and truly endless. It'll show obstinacy or no will at all. It'll be a sharp, pliant metaphor and the most boring thing in the world; annoyingly, sometimes both at the same time. In fact, it'll appear to be so many things, that the only safe truth about it will probably be what one sees before any serious thinking has started: water moving from one place to another. With the world beside it, it has a simple contract: it admits only that which has a past that's complete.

Stockholm Syndrome

I'd often seen the runway kissed by refugees
and bought-out hostages, an odd drunk and those
renouncing the flying for good, and thought
that surely there must be worse places to touch
freedom. Between the tailfins and the grey town
in the distance, gravity cropped up only at a newsstand,
and fizzled out with the first bite of the octane damp,
the view of the parking bunkers and stacked hovels
by the motorway. Everything else, before and after,
could have fitted into half a cigarette, the sickly sunshine
and endless nights, the flags and oaths (the very language
I wanted to forget), the Celts, the Saxons, the housebroken
Vikings in crowded trains, hopping frozen behind stalls
selling tat to tourists. Not enough time for loving because of
other loves, no codebooks or guides except the perennial
A to Z of not giving offense. The words were always there,
smooth like pebbles (soap on the tongue), and sometimes
the mockery of a commonplace, like that time when we put
up a blackened Union Jack instead of curtains between us
and the Poles on the scaffolding across the road.
On occasions it seemed good enough to be happy or scared
with the rest, to bring home from the terraces and parades
that sly acceptance, to sit in the shadow of atavism as under
a palm tree, and chew blissfully on the sweet dirt, the taste
of the crowd. Or for an evening make a shortcut through
someone else's work, an incomer's story of a homeland
gained not lost, a fat compendium of patriotic verse;
in essence, cheat again. In other words – never spend
too much on a suit rarely worn … If there had been
loyalty at all, it fell on faces and disappeared with them,
on promises and smiles, crazy schemes for finding

undiscovered shores. The world, I thought, could be unfolded
anywhere, if only you could fit it into a travel bag, into a clear,
irrevocable word. It is strange perhaps that even today
I think the same, still in the same place, buried firmly
like a rock in a graveyard, as heavy, and as pointlessly
decorated by lightness. The vows of yesterday skim
the heights like animal shapes we recognize in passing
clouds; postcards sleep in the unread books. Just like
the nomadic tribes used to, I learn of myself only
with my feet now, from the single map that remained.
And when streets bring the shortened future a bit nearer,
with open palm I seek the roughness of the facades,
and in the friendly pain I find the coarse, unperfected
truth of things. This, I think then, must be what it's like
in the bellies of gigantic animals: wet and quiet, almost
pleasant, once you get used to the smell of those who
passed through before you, and the immutable truth
that there is no going forward or anywhere else ...

Memory

Her dog, looking for his food,
still goes to the old spot, and taps the lino hazily
where the bowl used to sit before the new extension
rearranged the world, muzzle tight in the corner,
as if the habit's claim would effect the parting
of the units. *It's only because you're ancient, dear,*
she subtitles like a parent would, and I see
the mind in the old mutt, always going
to those same spooned-out places, following itself
like a truffle picker, and bringing back
an ever younger sibling of what was failure
to begin with, thinking that all else must still be
in its rightful place, because sun, leaf, cobweb
                                        and that smile
still flutter this side of the beaten trek ...

Dog-sitting

My friend's little dog in my garden,
for hours fixated on the top of the brick wall,
not at all on the garden itself

reminds me how, in a besieged city,
less and less I noticed the streets and the people,
until only the invisible fence remained.

The dogs were, I remember, calmer than us,
looking moderately disappointed, as if wanting
to shame without offending, lugging around

this same restrained sadness,
seemingly nothing to do with people
and all to do with the state of the world.

Maybe that's what saved their necks in the end
when there was no food left: a gift for mimicry,
a heart neither full nor empty.

Versions

Imagined, the places my father went fishing
teeter, not at all strangely, between the mute
and the faceless: a pastoral default, forest,
a shore edged in reed, a jetty stifling a creak
to hear, even there, those names read out
on the radio, as they changed hands in flames.

The arc between the idyll and hell, it seems,
is a finger pointed at something that still needs
working out, the cryptic absence of fishermen,
the sneaking up of the war on us ... An image
made by sidestepping it, and in that space –
a memory of someone, their glowing un-presence.

At nightfall, they'd come back with barely a fish
among them, abnormally happy, deliver Father
in a storm of kit clutter like a borrowed child
to parents, and it would, for a minute, take hold
of us all, the fishing vibe, the jokes somehow
better for the places they'd been ...

                         Nothing
was feigned, feared or imagined in that hallway,
and the meagre heart of it all still pumps out
the aromas of rubber and musty canvas into
this circumvented present. The other father
is a looming, coughing echo of expectations,

         a long ringing of the phone
to which neither Mother nor I dare bring our
thin excuses for the absconding fisherman,
and seared into the table a fresh, finger-long
sign of presence, a brown-burnished halo
where a cigarette dropped and was put out
by the sheer weight of darkness ...

Then and Now

If I go back I take one afternoon, and visit
the old neighbourhood, walk beneath our windows,
both sides of the building, as if looking to buy. More and more
it seems that I go for nothing else but for that feeling
of absolute dispossession, which sets in only there,
where two images of the street overlap
and make the sound of imperfect locking,
like two cogwheels crushing a finger.

Yesterday, on the way back, a pack of stray dogs went after me
and from a café people calmly observed over their cups,
me running away,
like I did in the same place twenty years ago
from snipers.

Jovo

No one, they say, throws
a surprise like death, and,
the family that we were,
I immediately think
of a cheat of sorts, our
grand-uncle Jovo, whose
first wife, along with the flat,
got repossessed in the war
by a local Nazi. Afterwards,
he chewed the soft and
the hard of life, always lugging
the same look, infinite
surprise, easy to mistake
for ebullience or lunacy.
Once, when I was ill,
by way of encouragement,
he told me that death is merely
a theft, a brazen operation
that, fortunately, occurs only
once in a lifetime, though –
a wink – not necessarily
at the end …

New Wave

No one knows where the villages begin, and the cantons
of melancholy stop; the lights and the language deceive,
they snake down the map like threads of spilt coffee
across the waxed paper.

People live under the ice of a mirror or wrapped
in newsprint. In summer, children pull plastic jewellery,
words and teeth from the caked mud; often,
the country is like a butcher's with no power.

The horoscopes are imported (the sky and the stars
deceive too); the sun is mostly good news, unless
someone asks for a debate on temperature.
Snow is part of the cultural heritage.

Branches sigh under the weighty thoughts
and sparrows award prizes for the loudest among them;
old men and empty brass heads in the park look on,
all adribble with pride.

In schools they teach that life is not a chasing after truth,
but submission, a fairytale about growing up. Dreams –
shabby, derelict leviathans – echo bluntly in the heads
touched only in passing by the holocaust.

To those once patient, time had become a burden;
the fat devour, the hasty rush, the wise go home
before dark. The mad – at least that hasn't changed –
are still troubled by metaphysics,

and the secret of survival, as always when big ideas die
a slow, undignified death, is carried into the future
by an obscure, tacky sect, in this case
the cabbies.

The important thing is, there is no hatred in murder, again
it's business only. The rivers are clean, technology redundant.
All ailments now have local solutions: a swig of theatre,
a rafting trip, sex without internet.

Refurbishment

Workers are removing the last traces of the war
from the flat, the shot-through blinds, the tiles patterned
with small-calibre holes. It's been this long because
Mother always felt like an intruder in Grandmother's old place,
waiting quietly for knick-knacks and sharp corners
to shift loyalty. Now it seems we've only been preparing
for another visit of the undertaker.

Across the road, the three skyscrapers hide the charring
and patchy masonry beneath laundry lines and satellite dishes;
who'd guess now that people once jumped off the burning floors?

New buses from the Czech Republic, new tenants
from villages razed to the ground;
the tidying up had only cleared space for more mess.
The papers again talk of fighting, history books hardly mention it.
Something, it seems, had jumped over our heads while we were looking
the other way, dragged itself forward from the past. Once again
death waits to be called in like a neighbourhood's only plumber,
and sieges brew in hand-me-down wars.

With Mother ...

I

In a conversation with Mother time stands still:
the two halves of the wall-clock are separated
by the meandering wartime crack. Our desert
under the building's white-hot roof is haunted by the tired,
familiar monsters: our dead, the wasted time, the war ...
We finally find ourselves where nothing counts: the treachery
of others, the loved ones, and we dig for that hidden nod
of collusion in every scrap still handy, fingering the past
like a cookery book. Once again, in our rehearsed nightmare
the voices of the long-gone speak in odd, forgotten words,
of sunlit moments, summer trips and birthday presents,
admitting no one and nothing into it, deaf to all else,
and in particular to matters like sour conscience or the petty crime
of survival. They give us party hats and dead carnations,
bleached bits of paper and old wrist-watches, and seem to
know us only when we take them. Both guilty, unpunished,
Mother and I still sit at the table, forever measuring
the useless plunder.

II

All those things words hug the way a half-blind
lovey-dovey drunk hugs a passer-by: 'an empty vessel,'
'a wounded bird,' 'a broken apparatus.' Cliché fits her,
like a glove: this life runs its dodgy heart out in a pointless testimonial,
lining up on the right for Thoughts Disunited against
the ever-hardy Speech City. She'd agree, of course, if
she heard it said, faithful to the last to that rampart
of least resistance, and again I would think that it's only
to spite me, if for nothing else. It hasn't been like that

at all; and it has been, forever: we never get to know who
they were before us anyway. A pile of rubble
in a bad, desperate disguise, held together by animal fear
and four brown walls, the memories of yesterday's lunch
eaten in 1945. Days throw a short shadow, and words
none at all. Still, we laugh. We laugh and wait
for someone else to stop the laughing. The laughter
is not the inheritance. The not stopping is.

Sarajevo

Laid out badly around comings and goings, the city
tells you once again: *You owe nothing, I gave you nothing;
or rather – you wanted nothing.* Then you size each other up like snipers
from the opposite sides of the river, trigger-muscles for an instant numbed
by the spring's warmth. You can't escape that, but it doesn't upset any longer;

only when you see the life grown over the remains of yours, you give in and
ask the images to speak up, as if they could. Once, remember, you believed
that if you stared long enough, you'd see yourself in the hurrying crowd;
only now you know that's impossible. What comes before the forgetting

is insecure about itself too: it pulls the sleeve from the dark, like hooks
jutting from the crumbling houses, long since not really sure themselves
what they were for. The last to admit the defeat, it's true,
                                                                         are the smells: of the thick
window paint, smog in the linen tablecloths. Someone, that much is clear,
has to fire first. The gunshot echoes in the world already altered, and only

the broken thought about the beauty of the spring that leaves the dead body
lingers a moment or two in the old one …